Thomas F. Yezerski

QUEEN OF THE WORLD

Farrar Straus Giroux • New York

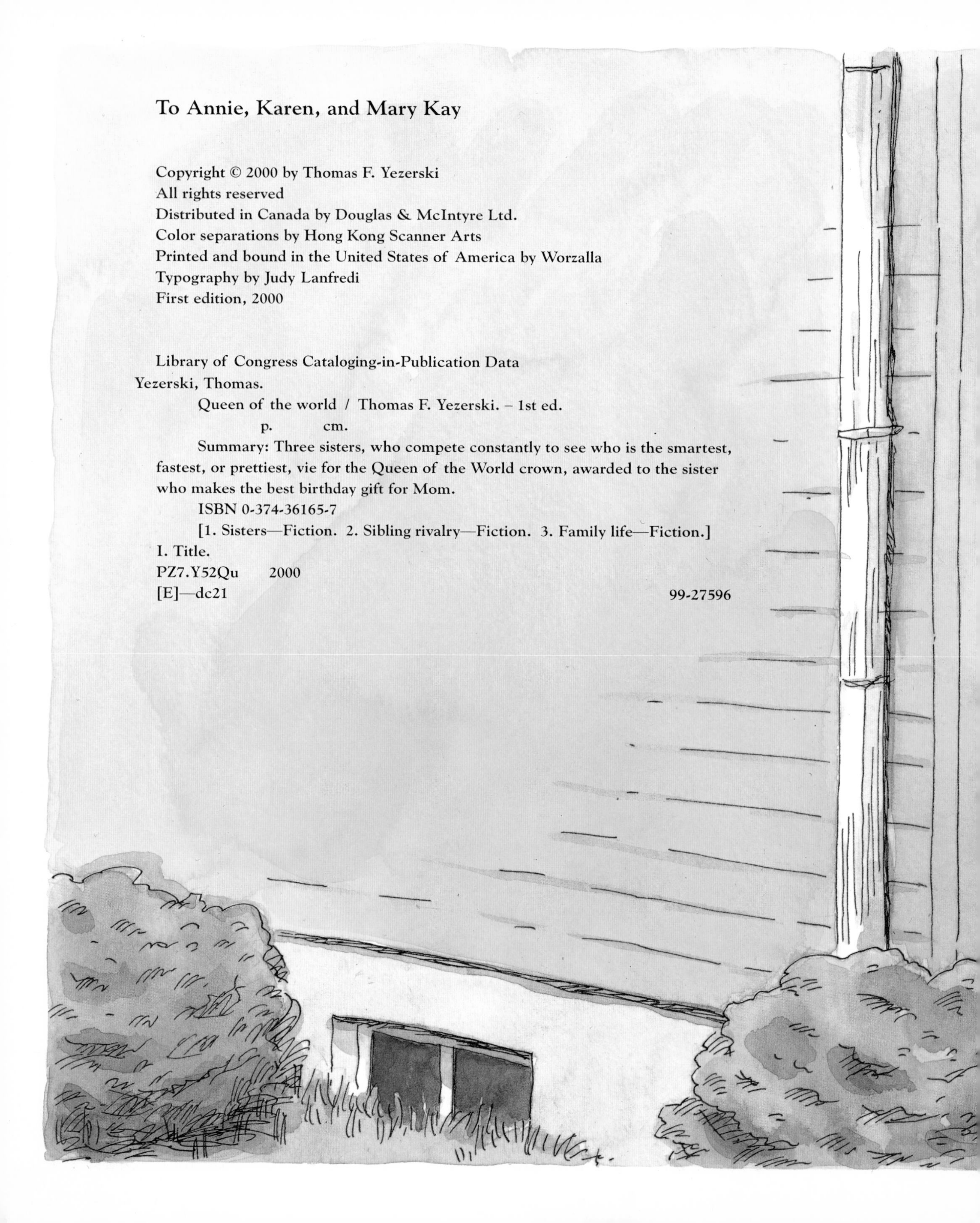

To Annie, Karen, and Mary Kay

Distributed in Canada by Douglas & McIntyre Ltd.
Color separations by Hong Kong Scanner Arts
Printed and bound in the United States of America by Worzalla
Typography by Judy Lanfredi
First edition, 2000

Library of Congress Cataloging-in-Publication Data
Yezerski, Thomas.
Queen of the world / Thomas F. Yezerski. – 1st ed.
p. cm.
Summary: Three sisters, who compete constantly to see who is the smartest, fastest, or prettiest, vie for the Queen of the World crown, awarded to the sister who makes the best birthday gift for Mom.
ISBN 0-374-36165-7
[1. Sisters—Fiction. 2. Sibling rivalry—Fiction. 3. Family life—Fiction.]
I. Title.
PZ7.Y52Qu 2000
[E]—dc21 99-27596

meeting
Tuesday 7
Mary the
BATON · TAP · JAZZ
DR. KAREN PARRIN
ORTHODONTIST
"Service for a smile!"
ANNIE BANANA
Are we there yet?!
Why don't you look out the window at the countryside. Enjoy the ride
OK.
But are we there yet?!

Like it or not, I have two sisters. Amanda is the oldest, Natalie is the youngest, and I am in the middle. Mom says all she wants is for us to get along—and maybe breakfast in bed, with tea the way she likes it. Dad says Mom has a good imagination.

My sisters and I try to get along, but sometimes it's just too hard.

Amanda, Natalie, and I aren't the same age. We don't do the same things, and we don't even like the same things. We do have to have the same room, though.

CIENCE MUSEUM

Sometimes, we try to play together . . .

. . . but we usually end up arguing. We argue about everything—about who is the smartest, or the strongest, or the prettiest, or just plain the best. Mom and Dad say they love us exactly the same, but what help is that?

Early one Saturday morning, Amanda, Natalie, and I were trying to figure out who was the loudest, when Dad came downstairs.

We thought we were in big trouble, but Dad just asked us to please keep it down, for Mom's sake, because it was her birthday. Mom's birthday? We had forgotten.

"Well, I'm going to make Mom the best present ever," said Natalie.

"No you're not. I am," said Amanda.

I knew they were both wrong, because my presents were always the best.

We were about to start fighting again, when I had an idea. "Let's have a contest!" I said. "We'll all make presents, and whichever one Mom likes best wins."

"And whoever wins will be Queen of the World!" said Amanda.

"Forever," added Natalie, "with no taking it back."

We made a crown for the winner. I drew its shape lightly in pencil on gold paper. Natalie carefully cut it out with the good scissors. Amanda wrote on it in bright red marker, in her fanciest handwriting, "Queen of the World."

We placed it in the middle of the kitchen table, for everyone to see.

"Look what a nice crown you made together!" said Mom. Amanda, Natalie, and I grinned at each other. Then we ran off to make the presents.

We each had our own ideas about what would make the best present, and we had to keep them secret.

We worked all day. We even forgot about lunch. It's not easy to become Queen of the World.

Wrapping the presents wasn't easy either.

But by suppertime we were ready.

It was a special night. Dad made salad and a pan of lasagna. There was a cake and lots of candles—for Mom's age. Everything was fine until Amanda touched me with her knee, and I had to pinch her under the table. Then Natalie flung a crouton at me for no reason.

Mom sighed. “Please be nice,” she said. But supper was over, and it was time to give Mom our presents.

"Oh, what have we here?" said Mom. "Which one shall I open first?"

We couldn't wait for her to decide, so we opened them for her.

"Which one do you like best?" I asked.

"Well," she said, "I love them all. You're the most generous daughters a mother could—"

"But mine's the best, right?" asked Natalie.

"Nooo it's not," said Amanda. "Mine is."

"Is not! Mine is!" I yelled.

Natalie grabbed the crown off the table and tried to get away.

"Give it!" "You dumbhead!" "Aaahhh!" we screamed.

There wasn't going to be a Queen of the World that night. Everything was quiet except for the dog chomping on Natalie's crouton. But then we heard something else.

It was the worst sound you could hear. Mom was crying—
not loud, not a lot—but she was crying. And it was our fault.

Dad wasn't crying, though. He was mad. He sent us to bed with no birthday cake, to think long and hard about what we had done.

We slunk upstairs, into our pajamas, and all the way up the ladder to the top bunk.

There we lay, together, as far away from what we had done as we could get.

"We made Mom cry," said Amanda.

"Yeah," said Natalie, as if she was going to cry, too.

"I feel terrible," I said. And I really did. We all did.

No Queen of the World makes her mom cry. We looked at the ceiling, wondering how we could make things right. And then we figured it out.

The next morning, Amanda, Natalie, and I got up before the sun itself. Like magic elves, we set to work on our plan.

We didn't have much time, and before long, we heard the tapping of the dog's tail upstairs, and then Dad's slippers shuffling. Amanda, Natalie, and I crept upstairs.

"Happy Birthday, Mom! Happy Birthday to the Queen of the World!" we shouted. We put the new crown on her head and served her a big breakfast in bed, with tea just how she likes it.

Mom hugged us and said it was exactly what she always wanted. It didn't matter that it wasn't her birthday anymore. What mattered was, we made her smile. Dad smiled, too, and so did we. I think even the dog was smiling.

Amanda, Natalie, and I still like different stuff and we still do different things. We'll never be the same age. We have one thing in common, though. We love our mom, and that's forever, with no taking it back.

ST. JOSE 'S COLLEGE CALLAHA LIBRARY
3 196

LIBRARY
'S COLLEGE
Avenue
ogue, NY 72-2399